I WISH

by Nancy Guettier

Illustrated by Meegan Barnes

I WISH

Illustrated by Meegan Barnes
Illustration copyright © 2015

Published in New York, New York, by Morgan James Publishing. Morgan James and The Entrepreneurial Publisher are trademarks of Morgan James, LLC. www.MorganJamesPublishing.com

The Morgan James Speakers Group can bring authors to your live event. For more information or to book an event visit The Morgan James Speakers Group at www.TheMorganJames-SpeakersGroup.com.

A **free** eBook edition is available
with the purchase of this print book.

CLEARLY PRINT YOUR NAME ABOVE IN UPPER CASE

Instructions to claim your free eBook edition:
1. Download the BitLit app for Android or iOS
2. Write your name in **UPPER CASE** on the line
3. Use the BitLit app to submit a photo
4. Download your eBook to any device

ISBN 978-1-63047-512-3 paperback
ISBN 978-1-63047-513-0 eBook
ISBN 978-1-63047-514-7 hardcover
Library of Congress Control Number:
2014921127

In an effort to support local communities and raise awareness and funds, Morgan James Publishing donates a percentage of all book sales for the life of each book to Habitat for Humanity Peninsula and Greater Williamsburg.

Get involved today, visit
www.MorganJamesBuilds.com

Habitat
for Humanity®
Peninsula and
Greater Williamsburg
Building Partner

This book is dedicated to my daughter Genevieve and her best friend Ariana.
I wish them both everlasting friendship and a lifetime of
sharing dreams, smiles, laughs and love.

This book is also dedicated to my mother and her wise words that
wishes really do come true, so make sure you wish for things you truly desire.

One day Genevieve and Ariana were playing by the pond.
Ariana looked down and found a magic wand.

She held it up high, gave it a twirl and a swish
and said, "I wish..."

"I wish I were a big fish
and I could swim deep in the blue sea.
That is what I wish I could be."

Genevieve looked down and said with a frown,
"But I would miss you here on land
because I could never hold your hand."

"Then I wish I were a big tall tree
and you could climb on me!"
Ari exclaimed with glee.

"Hmm, that could be fun," Genevieve said,
"but when the day is done you would have to sleep outside
instead of by my side."

Ari agreed and said,
"Then I wish I were a kitty cat and I could nap upon your lap."

"I would like that," Genevieve said,
"but when you awoke
you couldn't tell me about the dream you had,
and that would make me very sad."

"I got it!" said Ari. "I wish I were a ladybug and you could take me everywhere you go."

"That wish is a big no," said Genevieve. "I'd rather have a hug than a ladybug."

Ari got excited and said, "Ok, ok,
then I wish I were a pretty little bird.
I could sing you a song,
and you could dance along."

"This is true," said Genevieve.
"But there are so many things we couldn't do,
and that would make me blue."

"Well, then I wish I were the moon and you were a star.
Together we could light up the sky."

"Wow! Both of us up in the sky," Genevieve replied.
"I could give that one a try. But I don't think I would like to be
so far from home," she said with a moan.

"I know what would make you happy!
If I wished I could just be ME."

"Yes, that's it!
If you are you and I am me,
we could laugh, play, dream and be happy every day."

Then Genevieve took the wand.
She held it up high, and with a twinkle in her eye
she said, "I have a wish too!
I wish for a best friend forever, and I wish it to be YOU."

The End

Nancy Guettier

Nancy Guettier is an emerging author of children's books. She is also the Vice President of Visual Merchandising for Pottery Barn Kids and PBteen where she has worked for 12 years creating dream rooms for her customers.

Working in the kids and baby industry for over 20 years, Nancy wanted to use her creative skills to educate kids through her whimsical stories.

Nancy is also a mother of three beautiful children who inspire her every day to write and share her stories with kids everywhere.

Meegan Barnes

Meegan Barnes is an artist and illustrator with a diverse background in the editorial, fashion and music industries. She lives and works in sunny LA with her filmmaker hubby, their Jack Russell Terrier, Alvin, and scrappy street dog, Willis.

When not drawing or painting, Meegan can be found in the ceramics studio, at the beach or on a dance floor.

You can see more of her work at www.meeganbarnes.com

Check out some of Nancy's other titles...

Roy G. Biv Is Mad At Me Because I LOVE PINK!

This is a delightful story of a girl named Genevieve who LOVES PINK! While splashing around in the puddles after a rain shower, she meets ROY G. BIV. He is upset because she only loves pink and pink is not a color in his rainbow. They have a fun encounter and Roy tries to convince Genevieve to give all the colors of the rainbow a try.

Mermaids On Mars

Mermaids On Mars is a whimsical story of a time when mermaids ruled Mars! A long time ago, Mars had the perfect environment for mermaids to thrive. They loved splashing around in the crater pools until one day they used up all the water supply. The mermaids had no choice but to take a rocket ship to earth where they now live in our oceans. The mermaids share their story and ways kids can conserve water here on earth.

more titles...

Jude's Moon

This is a story of a little boy named Jude who loves the moon. One day after noticing a crescent moon for the very first time, he discovers the different phases of the moon and how its appearance changes as it travels with the earth around the sun..

Circus In The Sky

This is a sweet story of a little boy named Julian who dreams he is the ring leader of the constellations. Throughout the evening, he discovers the magic of the night sky and meets the winged-horse Pegasus, Leo the Lion, the Gemini twins and more!

Wishes really do come true, so make sure you wish for things you truly desire.

CPSIA information can be obtained at www.ICGtesting.com
Printed in the USA
BVOW11*1308300415

397951BV00002B/2/P